# Love
## WITH A
# Stranger

# Love
## WITH A
# Stranger

Another journey to find true love

# Cara Carón

XULON PRESS

Xulon Press
2301 Lucien Way #415
Maitland, FL 32751
407.339.4217
www.xulonpress.com

Paperback ISBN-13: 978-1-66281-968-1
Ebook ISBN-13: 978-1-66281-969-8

# Acknowledgements

To All Those Souls
Who Contributed
The Beautiful Moments
That Make My Heart
Sing

Love is a canvas furnished by nature
and embroidered by imagination
… Voltaire

# TABLE OF CONTENTS

# Chapter 1

# THREE GIRLS REUNITE

What to do on a rainy day? Guess I'll give Lisa a call and see if she wants to go to Brown fitness. We really do need to work out. We used to go every day and recently we've been kind of cheating. I guess I'll give her a call.

"Hey Lisa, how about us going to Brown fitness today? You know we need to stay in good shape, being we are still single."

"Now Laura, you know I'm not single."

"You might as well be, he'll never come to the gym. Lisa, meet me down there in an hour, okay?"

"Yeah, I guess I can do that."

Lisa got there before me. When I came through the door, she started waving to me to come over there. She was talking to her friend Dan. I have to say, I had never met him, but I enjoyed him. Once Lisa introduced me to Dan, she left and went on the treadmill. I wanted to go on some other machines. Dan and I were going to the same machines. We started to work out and when we took a break, Dan suggested we go out for lunch after the gym.

Lisa agreed and the three of us went to Bella's Café. Dan had gone to Yale too. He graduated a year after Lisa and me. Lisa's husband, Bill was a Yale alumnus too. We started talking about one thing and another and Dan had an idea.

"You know we really should get a reunion going. I really miss a lot of the people we used to see in college."

Lisa and I did not think much of the idea. I told Dan we would think about it. The next day, Lisa said when she told her husband, he thought that might be a great idea. I told Lisa I would have to think about it.

About a week later, Lisa called me and was telling me about a conversation she and Dan had.

"Do you remember a girl, named Ann Marie Anderson?" Dan asked.

"You have got to be kidding. Laura, Ann and I were a threesome all through college. She later got married and moved away. We lost touch," I answered.

Dan said, "My friend, Todd and I were talking the other day, and he said that he kept in contact with her because he was friends with her husband John. He told me that Ann had had a miscarriage and later, John and she got divorced."

"I just can't believe it. I thought they were madly in love. It's sad to hear she had a miscarriage." Laura said.

"I then asked Dan, do you think you could get her phone number from Todd? I am beginning to think the reunion is a really good idea. There are so many people that I enjoyed in college and have not seen since. He told me she lived in New York City. I couldn't wait to talk to her and find out the whole story. I called Ann, but there was no answer. I left my callback number and reminded her of who I am and told her to call me when she got the chance." Lisa commented.

"I will call her later today; I can't wait to hear." Laura said.

Ann reached Laura. She couldn't believe we knew Dan and Dan knew Todd. Small world, isn't it? She was glad to step back in time to when we three, Lisa, Ann and I were the three who were always together.

"Dan told us you are single again, Ann."

"It's complicated. Maybe we can get together real soon. I would love to hear all about what's going on with you and Lisa. Are you guys married?"

"Ann, Lisa is, at least for the moment, but not me. I am dating someone. Can you come to New Haven next weekend?"

"Laura, I will need to call you back; I'm not sure yet. I could have a date, but I'd rather come to see you two."

Thursday Ann called and was able to come to town.

Lisa and I picked Ann up at the airport. We didn't recognize her. She was thin.

"Girl we need to feed you some crème puffs."

We hadn't seen each other for years; we looked different to Ann too.

"Let's go to the Shake Shack for some lunch," Laura suggested.

We got seated and Lisa started in.

"Ann, you go first. We wanna hear what happened," Lisa said.

"Well, where do I begin. I am still figuring life out. I was already pregnant. John and I had no honeymoon. He had quit his job the day before we got married and started a new job the following Monday. I started missing days at work. One day I started to feel awful and went to the doctor. Next day I had a miscarriage. What a way to begin a marriage. After about six months, we seemed to be at odds all the time. John wanted me to be on the phone or with him every minute. He became possessive. When we dated, he was never like that. Now he didn't want me to go out with my girl-friends. They were all single and I guess he was afraid

4

I'd meet somebody else. I thought it was flattering that he always wanted to be with me. At first, I didn't realize how controlling he was being. The girls kept reminding me to speak up. I recently had lost the baby and it's not my way to be confronting. Eventually I started to have bladder and kidney infection all the time. My doctor suggested I might see a psychologist. I decided to try to deal with this myself. After about a year and trying to talk with John, I realized he could not communicate. I suggested we go our separate ways. He became angry. I got an apartment, and the rest is history. I never want to deal with men going forward. Okay I have told you guys my life's story now let's enjoy lunch. I can stay until Tuesday."

"Wow, no wonder you look so thin. How's your mom Marie?" Lisa asked.

"Oh, she was my lifeline through all my trauma. She's great. She thought I might stay in New York City, thinking I could have a new start."

"Tonight, we are going to Club Vandome. They have some great music. You can come down and let loose," Laura suggested.

"Tomorrow I want to hear all your stories," Ann said.

"After we leave here, let's you two go to Laura's and put your luggage there and show you your room, Lisa said. I will pick you two up at nine to go to the Club. Ann, ride with Laura and I will go to my place. See you at nine."

"I hope you like my place, Ann. It's not a palace, but the price is right. I still have my college loan."

"Laura, I am glad to be here with old friends. I needed these few days as a relief from my real life. I did not bring any dress up clothes for tonight."

"Ann you can go in my closet, I'm sure you will find something. We are about the same size. Let's order some food in for lunch, so we can talk. How about some Chinese?"

"Love it."

Ann what happened with you and John?"

"You don't think that it's not all about you. My parents were in love always and that's what I wanted. At first, John only wanted to be with me. My friends would want to go out with us, but he didn't want to go. He said that he wanted to be with me. Perfect. He was overly critical. His mother had cheated on his father, once and then his father never trusted her again. I could never do anything right. John carried that baggage that he would never let his woman out of his site. At the time, I didn't know all that. I don't know but maybe the stress caused me to miscarry. If I had seen clearly, it was all there. I wanted love so much, I overlooked a lot. My parents were so into each other that I sometimes felt like an outsider. Maybe it was my perception, but it did affect my decisions. I had to leave. I was getting sick constantly with bladder and kidney infections. Once I left, I never was sick again."

"Does that make you feel it's more difficult to get into a new relationship?" Laura asked.

"I don't even want to think about going through that again."

"Lisa should be here shortly to pick us up, we better get ready. Tonight, we need to go and have fun."

We heard her lay on the horn.

"That's Lisa. She could have texted us, but no, she's a piece of work." Laura quipped.

We arrived about nine thirty. The music was loud, the dance floor was full, and we were set for a great night. We danced and drank until two in the morning.

Lisa dropped us off at my house and we crashed. We agreed to meet Saturday in the afternoon.

We got up late Saturday morning.

"We are taking you to Artspace today, Ann. I know you as an artist, will enjoy their works. Are you still teaching at NYC?" Laura asked.

"Yes, John and I both got jobs at NYC, that's how we ended up moving to New York. After the miscarriage, I had to get back to work to keep me going."

"Sounds like Lisa is here. Come on in. Let's stop for a sandwich at Claire's before the gallery."

"Heh, you two what did I miss? Ann, I need to catch up too. Remember Kurt from college. We recently reconnected and we do have fun."

"Let's get this show on the road," Laura suggested.

We got to Claire's and Lisa took over the conversation. She thought she had missed something. We ordered before Lisa got a chance to take over.

"Okay, Ann give me the scoop. How come you got divorced?" Lisa asked.

"Lisa, it wasn't that way. We agreed, he would never trust me due to his baggage and I couldn't live with that. We went to counseling that's how I found out, first then that he had issues from his parent's deal. I decided to stay at NYC and continue working there. My mom thought I might move back home, but no way. I needed my space."

"Lisa, how's your love life working?" Ann asked.

"Bill had been in several relationships before me. He often mentions how this one or that one did things. I told him to have at it and go be with them if that's what he likes. You know me. I am my own woman. No man is going to tell me what to do or not. I think I have about had it. He is tons of fun, but not for a real relationship. Laura's the one who has a great guy. He knows how to treat a woman. He's such a steady eddy. Of course, Laura you think he's boring."

"Everyone is looking for different things. I am not marrying him. Jim's okay for now. Let's leave now, before we get into it." Laura said.

Artspace had a local artist featured, Key Jo Lee this weekend. Ann was more than thrilled. She was in her element. Ann has always been an abstract fan. We three were happy to get to spend time with each other.

*Chapter 2*

# REUNION

Sunday, we had our get together with the three of us and we invited Dan and Kurt, Lisa's friends. We decided to talk about the reunion we would plan.

Dan suggested that Laura oversee getting a list of names and addresses. Lisa would plan the theme and decorations. The guys would help as needed. Ann was the only one from out of town, so we would have to delegate where she could help. The sketch was outlined for the event. We had not decided a location. The guys had to leave for a five o'clock game. We decided to get a pizza from Sally's. They have the best in town. We agreed to get the pizza with the works.

Ann asked, "Lisa, what are you going to do with Bill and you?"

"We got married last year. The truth is my parent's felt I was too picky and that no man could meet my standards. Finally, I cowered to their idea. Bill was a real nice guy and I thought maybe this is as good as it gets. I married him. The wedding didn't go that well.

His mother had hurt feelings by one of my friends. She mistook the conversation. I went to the restroom and was in tears. I feel like it's time to separate. I try to talk with him, but because his family argued so much, he would never sit down and discuss anything. He would get incredibly quiet."

"Lisa that sounds familiar to me. I right now am tired of men in general. I at this time anyway, don't want to be in a relationship," Ann replied.

"Laura, you seem to be the only one of us that has a good relationship," Lisa said.

"Believe none of what you hear and only half of what you see, Lisa. Jim keeps the place neat as a pin. He expects me to do the same. If I leave the curling iron out, he complains. Now how to put a hot curl iron away. One fork in the sink, he fusses. I keep a decent place, but he needs perfect. I am not good with the checkbook, another issue. He says how could you not do something that simple? It gets old, quick. He is totally not a romantic. Same old stuff in bed every night, nothing new, just get it done. I really need some romance. At least we are not married."

Lisa comes up with a new idea. "Maybe you two should go online. That way you could try him out without him being in the room. You could ask all your questions ahead of meeting him."

Ann says, "No way Jose. I do not want a man right now, maybe never. I need my freedom."

"I would consider the thought. It's about time for me to get the real thing," Laura quipped.

"Let's get off the subject guys and go to a movie tonight," Lisa spoke up.

"What's playing at Bow Tie Criterion tonight? Laura asked. It really doesn't matter if we get out."

Lisa says. "I will meet you there."

It was a funny movie. We were pop corned out as we left. Lisa had to work Monday, and she went on home.

Ann and I talked to the wee hours of the morning. We didn't have much sleep but got up at six and had some coffee and a bagel. We left at seven and hugged at the airport. Ann promised to come back again soon. I could see she had a tear in her eye.

"I promise it won't be long. I really need to play more. It's been a trip being alone again."

About a month went by and I was having difficulty finding our classmates, so called Ann.

Lisa was busy getting a theme and decorations for the event. Dan called. He and Kurt found a great hall, at Amarante's Sea Cliff. He said,

"You can dance, a huge dance floor, big hall and you can go outdoors and down to the water if you like."

The date was now set for July 21. Everything was falling in place. Ann was able to come to town for the week before the event to help.

*Chapter 3*

# CHANGE IN PLANS

*U*nbelievable, I got a call from Lisa that Bill was killed in a car crash on the way home from the airport. He was coming home from a business trip. She could barely speak. Lisa's parents lived in Florida so could not be there. What a shock. None of us were ready for that news. I ran over to Lisa's to be with her. She was inconsolable. I called our friends to let them know. How sad we all were. I stayed overnight and on the next day Lisa's parents got tickets to come to New Haven.

Good thing Ann had such artistic ability because she had to take over Lisa's tasks. Lisa is always ahead of the game, so almost everything was ready. In this circumstance, Lisa could barely function.

Her parents flew in from Naples. Her mom made the arrangements for a service. Bill's parents came in also. Lisa's parents were able to stay a week or so to get Lisa back on her feet.

Ann took over Lisa's role and did a fantastic job. It was a fabulous weather weekend. While it was still light everyone gathered outside and down by the water. In the evening people had changed clothes and were ready to party. The band was versatile and took requests. Everyone was on the dance floor at some point. We took a lot of pictures so when Lisa felt more like it, she would be able to enjoy the pictures. People sure had changed over years. It was our five-year reunion.

Ann was staying at my place, but that night we stayed at The Blake where most guests were booked, just to be with our friends later and not worry if we drank too much.

Ann had to teach on Tuesday, so she was flying out on Monday early. I drove her to the airport and we both promised to keep in touch with Lisa. Once Lisa's parents went back to Florida, I started to drop in on Lisa more often. Good thing her hair salon was busy, she didn't have much time to think of her own problems.

Lisa had been planning to sell the salon and now that business was great, it was easier to sell. Susie had rented a chair in the salon and was doing well. She approached Lisa and asked what her selling price would be. Lisa really liked Susie and wanted to give her a break.

Bill's life insurance policy really helped Lisa financially. She and Susie worked out a deal and Susie became the new owner of Le Salon. Lisa needed a total break to reinvent her life and decided to sell her house and go down to Naples and stay with her parents for a while. The house sold fast, and Lisa came over to my house and we cried and hugged and said our goodbye's.

# Chapter 4

## ELITE SINGLES

About a month later, Ann called me and said she would be coming to New Haven on the weekend. I was glad to hear from her. Dan and Kurt decided to come over on Saturday to see Ann and we decided to go to Sally's for pizza Saturday night. Jim was playing in a soccer tournament; it all worked out well. We reminisced about the fun we had at the reunion and how different people looked. The guys left and Ann and I went to my house. We talked to near morning. Sunday Ann came up with an idea.

"Laura, do you remember when Lisa came up with this crazy idea of going online? I thought she had lost her mind, but now it's been some time and I think that I may be ready."

"Ann I never thought I would hear that coming out of your mouth, but I think it's not a bad idea. I think we should look up to see what site we'd like to go on first. I found this site I thought we might try called Elite Singles."

"My heart is already pounding just thinking about it. We need to find some good pictures of ourselves to put on the site. Laura, help me with setting up my profile and then I will help you. Let's each write our story for our profile and then I'll read yours and you read mine."

"This might be the craziest thing we've done in a while, but what the heck. Nothing ventured nothing gained." Laura said.

We each found the right picture and then we each screened the other's profile. It took us a while, but we got our profiles and pictures online.

"Ann, do you know it's two o'clock and your flight takes off early tomorrow?"

"You must be kidding. I can't believe how long this took to accomplish. It's worth it though because we're ready to rock-n-roll."

Monday morning, Ann had a cab to pick her up to go to the airport. She promised and I promised we would talk as soon as we got a hit on our site.

Ann called me on Thursday to share the events of the week on her site. She already had twenty hits. She said so far none of them tripped her trigger. I told her that I had fifteen hits. Their profiles were wearisome. We both agreed to stay on for a few months to entertain ourselves. We were both busy at our jobs for a while and neither one of us looked at the site.

# Chapter 5

# ENTER EGIDIO

*A*nn called me shrieking.

"OMG, you won't believe this one. This guy looks like an Adonis. We started texting back and forth, just a few lines at first, and now it's every day. It's starting to scare me because I had heard about Catfishes and my mother always warned me because of course you know Laura, that my grandmother left me quite a bit of money. If anything, ever happened to my parents, God forbid, being an only child, I probably would get their money also. My mother's words ring in my ears. I figured nothing to lose by going online because I'm not going to see them. Guess what, he asked me where I live, and I answered New York City." He responded,

"How interesting. I'm in New York City also."

"Next, he tells me he went to Yale, believe that or not."

"Ann, what's this guy's name?"

"You ready Laura, Egidio, don't know if that's Italian or French, sounds Italian."

"My news is a little different. I haven't had much time to go online because Jim and I are having issues. He's such a great guy however I realized it's near impossible for me to stay with a man who has no emotion. I thought I would take stability over romance, but I realize I need both. I believe by next month; we will break up. I think Jim already realizes that I'm about to go. Maybe tonight I'll look at my profile and see what's going on. I'll call you if anything interesting is happening. I want you to keep me informed on this new adventure of yours. Call me next week and let me know your progress. By then I would think you'll either love him or hate him."

"It's all a bit scary to me since he lives in the same city I do. He feasibly could come over here. Right now, I want to know more about him and who he really is. He seems very professional and very cultured, which I love. He tells me he's not an artist however he appreciates fine art. He seems to love Europe as my grandmother always did. I loved Paris when I visited her, but that's all I know about Europe."

Laura said, "You Ann, of all of us will handle it. Sounds interesting though."

*Chapter 6*

# GIRLS RECONNECT

*I*t seemed all our friends had their own agendas. We didn't get together much or hear from one another. It had been several months and then I saw a text from Lisa. She decided to come back to New Haven where her heart was. I couldn't have been more thrilled because we were always tight. By now I had broken it off with Jim. I was excited that maybe Lisa, Ann and I could go out some. Lisa called,

"I will be coming to New Haven in about three weeks."

I told her I would get in touch with Ann and see if the three of us could have a girl's weekend. She was thrilled with that. I was busy at work so I just texted Ann that Lisa would be coming home in three weeks and that Ann should think about coming in that weekend. I didn't get a chance to tell her about Jim and me. I figured we three girls would talk girl talk when we got together.

All worked. Lisa came in and Ann flew in and we three college friends were ready to reconnect. Each had had a change in their lives. I suggested we all stay at my apartment. I had a two bedroom, and my sofa was a sleeper. We all agreed. Great decision. We had food delivered because each of us needed to share and were exhausted. Lisa had come a long way as her parents were supportive and Lisa was a futurist. She was brought up to deal with what is and move on. She did. Kurt had called Lisa recently and said that he still thinks about her and he is still single.

Laura said, "I was glad I had the wherewithal to leave a man I loved, but for both of us, I had to let the birds fly, even if in different directions."

We were both anxious to hear Ann's new story. It got late so Ann said that we should close shop and she would tell us her story tomorrow.

None of us could wait for morning. We got up and decided to go for bagels at Brueggers. Lisa looked so different. She was back to her college self. She was a different person than when she was married. She was calm. A new thing for Lisa. Ann had a glow. We couldn't wait to hear her online romance.

We got back to my apartment. We decided to stay home today and catch up. It was Ann's turn to give it up.

"Okay what's the smirk on your faces? It's up to twice some days that we text. The latest is, he wants to get together. That really shakes me to my toes," Ann said.

Lisa asks, "What's the hang-up, you really like him?"

"That's the exact problem. I want to keep my head on and not let my heart take over."

"Couldn't you meet him somewhere for coffee?" Lisa asked.

"Yeah, I know me too well. I sometimes get too involved too soon."

"You already are silly girl," Laura said.

"I told him I would let him know when I come back to New York. He wants to take me to dinner at Balthazar. I had to look it up. It's a fancy place. John never cared that much about dining. It's a lot for me to think about. I feel safer meeting him at lunch or coffee."

"He sounds at least to not mind spending some change. I heard of Balthazar's. It's one of the top restaurants in New York. I never went there, but I have heard about it," Lisa chimed in.

"It scares the life out of me. Too good to be true. I hear my mother's voice. Be careful. You have money and they may have looked you up somehow."

"Ann, with that mindset, you will be always single," Lisa stated.

"Wow Ann, you know Jim and I are no longer. Now I will have to check what is happening on Elite. Maybe men are dying to meet me, Ha ha. I haven't looked in a month. I wanted to get you going, not me. Lisa have you ever thought about going online or is it too soon, you were the one who got us started, way back when."

"I am interested in Kurt right now, Laura. Let's see how you two fare and maybe I will look for true love if it exists. You two prove it to me first."

We had a fun time, the three of us and then Ann had to fly back. Lisa could stay, as she was looking for an apartment in New Haven.

We told Ann to keep us informed of the love life she was denying. She promised. We didn't think she would share.

It was only a couple of weeks and Ann texted me to call her. It didn't take me long to call. I was anxious to hear, good or bad.

"You won't believe it. I got flowers today, somehow, he found my address. The card just said, "Merci." Now I am frightened. He knows where I live."

"Ann be careful, but getting flowers is romantic," Laura warned.

"I really like everything we talk about, but I never did anything like this."

"Maybe it's time you did."

"Gotta go, my land line is ringing."

## Chapter 7

# BON JOUR, ANN

"Hello, Ann speaking."

"Bon Jour Ann."

"Who is this?"

"Egidio"

"How did you get this number?"

"It is a public number. I read your article in the New York Times. I didn't know you wrote for them. I want so much to see you."

"Only lunch and I will meet you there."

"If that's what you prefer, Ann. Meet you at Bab's Wednesday at 1:30. Does that work for you?"

"Wednesday will work."

"Looking forward to see your beautiful face."

I called Laura immediately after I hung up.

"Laura, you won't believe what just happened. He called me. That was him on the phone. I told him I would only meet him for lunch. My heart is beating out of my chest. Scared, happy, excited all at one time."

"Calm down girl. Sounds fantastic. When are you going?"

"Wednesday afternoon."

"Call me with the details. I have to work late Wednesday but call me Thursday."

Once I hung up, reality set in. I got excited to see him and what to wear. I hadn't felt this alive and happy in a long time. Was I getting into another relationship as much as I had to convince myself it was just to pass the time? Now another person's feeling was involved. I had to be me so he could decide if he wanted to be with me, for me. I had to make the assessment.

Wednesday finally came and I had only seen a head-shot that we exchanged. I didn't know his height, weight and so forth. We had had much to talk about, I forgot to think about those details. There he was right outside the door. Wow and wow!!! He was all that tall, dark, great physique. I was breathless. He grabbed me and gave me a tight hug. He seemed speechless too. He opened the door, and we went in. They called him by name, he evidently was here frequently. I wondered who he might have brought here in the past. I am always suspicious of men. The restaurant was stunning all gold and black.

"All I can do is keep my eyes on you Ann. You are a beautiful woman. Your long black hair frames those stunning brown eyes. I am fortunate you agreed to come this afternoon."

"Thank you Egidio. I am glad I accepted your invite."

We were seated near the windows.

He kept looking in my eyes, it made me nervous, although I already had my own set of butterflies. We looked over the menu.

"You might enjoy the crab BLT. I have enjoyed it before. However, have whatever you like," Egidio offered.

After a special time at lunch, we liked each other even more.

"Ann, would you have time to go for an ice cream?"

We both didn't want to leave each other this soon.

"I haven't had a cone in forever, yes," Ann smiled.

I ordered butter pecan and he ordered fudge ripple. He handed me an extra napkin as my cone was dripping.

"I hope this means we can see each other again. I'd like to take you to Balthazar's on Saturday evening, but I would want to pick you up at your home if you agree."

I didn't answer for a bit and he looked disappointed.

"Would that hesitation I see be a, no?"

"I'm on overwhelm. It's all so much, so soon. You have my home number, call me tomorrow." I promise to give you an answer."

"You know it's going to be a yes, I look forward to the call." He smiled.

We hugged. He kissed me on the cheek, and we parted. I got home and he already texted.

He said,"I had a beautiful time with you today and can't wait until you say yes to Saturday evening. You are a dream come true for me. I hope you care also. Waiting on your response." Always, Egidio

I thought I better not answer too soon. I didn't want to seem needy. I already had made up my mind to go.

Next evening, I looked at my phone, Another message from Egidio.

"I will pick you up at seven o'clock on Saturday. Waiting for you to say yes."

He really is sure of himself. I personally like that about a man, but I know 1 need to keep my feet on the ground.

Friday, I felt I had held him off long enough, I texted him and said,

"Seven will be fine. Give you directions."

My apartment has a locked entry, I gave him the code.

Saturday night he came with a bouquet of white cymbidium orchids. He was taking me to a fine restaurant and giving me orchids, now my mind thought he is pretending he is rich and then what when I find out who he really is. I always think of those catfishes. Guess I should settle down. He is such a gentleman, and we enjoy many ideas and art and culture and both of us enjoy Europe. I told him about my trip to see grandma in Paris and he said he had been there. He had come in a cab. Parking in New York is nonexistent.

Saturday evening was enchanting. I feel we both had stars in our eyes. He ordered a bottle of Pinot Grigio, and I enjoyed the Salmon. Egidio had the Trout. We shared a plate of Pavlova with strawberries. He put the fork up to my mouth, I melted. After dinner he dropped me at the front door, and we kissed goodnight as his cab was waiting.

# Chapter 8

# Is Love in the Air?

Sunday, I had to call Laura.

"Laura, I need you to put my feet back on the ground. I am floating. He is good looking. He has such a charming demeanor and has a slight accent. He has lived in New York since college. He is a graphic designer. He seemed fascinated by me."

"Ann let it unfold. Life is made of moments and if you can have some good times, enjoy the ride with your eyes open. I started to respond to some of the men online, interesting but this far no great catches. Lisa is still seeing Kurt."

Egidio called Sunday night. We texted every day. He suggested we start doing Facetime. I was anxious to be able to get a glimpse of his place. I agreed. I was working more hours writing. I was teaching at NYC by day and writing into the night. Hard to find time for texting Egidio. He started questioning if I was losing interest. Only so many hours in the day. He could come and go in my life, but I needed to oversee my life going smooth.

"Look forward to spending more time with you next weekend," Egidio said.

"Merci, it was a splendid evening, I agree. Gotta go and we'll talk soon."

I was getting more assignments, they seemed to like my work. That evening Egidio wanted to stop over, but again I was under deadlines. He talked about the more he sees me, the more he wants to be with me. We phone kissed and I stayed up way late to get this article done.

I feel there is a possibility I could quit teaching and keep freelancing. Writing and my art are my passions. The writing makes money, and the art brings me satisfaction.

We agreed to get together on the weekend. Egidio and I were seeing as much of each other as our schedules allowed. We went to the theatre as often as a play we would enjoy was available. We both enjoyed fine dining. Egidio seemed to know every place in town, and they all seemed to call him by first name. I wondered if he was a player and who had he brought to these places before.

I thought it's about time to call Laura. Seemed Egidio was taking all my spare time.

Laura answered, "Oh the dead live?"

"I am sorry, I have neglected our friendship. Guess I got lost in the sea of love."

"Did you say love, Ann?"

"I mean I really like him so much, it's frightening. I remember my mom's words, "Be Cautious." So far the only thing I see is that wherever we go everyone knows him."

"Ann, maybe this is for real. Things like that DO happen."

"How are you doing online, or did you give up?"

"Actually, I met a genuinely nice guy last week. We are texting quite often. I don't know yet though. Lisa is back in New Haven now and has a nice apartment and is seeing Kurt. It sounds like that relationship is good for now. She decided to open a nail salon. It's right next door to the hair salon she used to have. They share customers. Hair and nails, great combo."

## Chapter 9

# A Weekend Getaway

"*E*gidio and I are going away for the weekend. I can't believe it, but I have now known him for four months. I had a hard time agreeing because you know what that means. I feel we are ready. He was always ready, but he did understand my hesitation. I told him about John and the miscarriage. He said that he would be considerate this weekend and be kind and gentle with my feelings. He's tender and special."

"Remember, Ann keep those feet on the ground. I can tell you are in love. Admit it or not. Do not set yourself up for hurt. Where are you going?" Laura asked.

"To the Jersey shore."

"Laura, who's your new friend? What's his name?"

"Peter and so far, so good. I am interested in him. He has an unusual job. He owns a funeral home. Funnier than that, his father is a taxidermist. Maybe not so hysterical.

I could be rubbing his shoulders and give him a great massage. With my massage job, I keep people healthy, and he takes care when life is done."

"What's Lisa up to with the man situation?" Ann asked.

"Guess Lisa isn't tied to Kurt anymore. She is semi interested in one of her clients. He comes in every other week for a manicure. He is a CPA. From what she told me he sounds a little quiet. His name is Gerald. You know how accountants are cut and dried. He is quite calm and just what she needs, Lisa says. Have a great time at the Shore. Will talk when you get back, that is if you're willing to share."

Egidio picked me up. I had reserved the only guest space in the garage. He carried my luggage. He came in his red Mazda Miata convertible. Glad I had my hair in a ponytail. It was a balmy, windy day. He did pick a great hotel. It was the Claridge. We went to the room. He grabbed me, kissed me and threw me on the bed.

"I think we should go to the beach darlin'," I insisted.

We got into some casual clothes and walked the beach. He dipped his hand in the water and splashed me. We laughed and kissed along the beach. It was lunch time, and we didn't want to go inside. We stopped at Mud City Crab House. We shared crab cakes. It was a warm day. He reached for my hand and suggested,

"How about we go to the Hotel Lobby and have a Frangelico?"

We sat and chatted about how good it was to get-away. He wanted to go to our room.

"Come on, let's go. I am not the bad guy, okay?"

The room was elegant. The comforter and shams were a pink and white floral and greens leaves.

He took me by the hand and led me to the bed.

"You are the most beautiful woman I have ever met. Your silken hair, your slim figure and especially those big brown eyes that glitter. I want to hold you close so I know it's real. I want to kiss every inch of your face and neck. I just want to lie and look at you. I appreciate your exquisite beauty."

We dosed off and next thing I know, Egidio was sitting in a chair with a drink in his hand.

"I didn't want to wake you. I wanted to take you all in, lying there so peaceful. Is it okay I made reservations for dinner at eight? We're dining at The Poached Pear."

I was quiet. I was overwhelmed and smiled and blinked my eyes at him. He came darting over to me, landed on the bed and rolled over and hugged and kissed me.

"Would you like a little Bailey's before you shower?"

"Oh yes, great."

We sat and talked and then I looked at the clock.

"I better shower. It takes me a while to do my hair."

We had discussed the weekend, before we left. I did have heels and a nice dress.

I came out and he gasped.

"I never thought you could look better. You look angelic. I can't get over your shiny long hair and that dress accentuates your every curve."

My dress was a black spaghetti strap, and rather short. I had black strappy heels. I don't do jewelry much but had a silver bracelet. He had black pants, black t-shirt and camel jacket. His hair was unusually wavy tonight.

"I need to say Egidio, you take my breath away. You are incredibly special to me."

"Let's go before we don't."

Dinner at The Poached Pear was an extravaganza. Not only was the food delicious, but the presentation was best bar none. I had sesame crusted Ahi Tuna. He had Octopus.

After dinner we shared Tiramisu.

Time to go back to the hotel. I threw my shoes off and sat in the big chair. We reminisced about our day. Egidio put his hand out and I grasped it. He led me to the bed.

"Hold on baby, I need to take off my dress." It didn't take much for him to make an offer.

"I would be more than happy to assist you."

He unzipped me and he pulled my smokey grey hose off.

"Just trying to be helpful."

I went to the restroom to get my gown on. I came out and he was already under the covers in anticipation. I could tell by the glint in his eyes, I wondered if he had anything on under the covers. I got in bed on my side, and he rolled over and squeezed me gently and kissed me.

"What did I do to deserve a beautiful woman like you?" He stroked my long dark hair, stroked my face and tapped on each eye lid.

"Mon Coeur, come into my arms. I want to hold you until morning. His lips touched mine, but barely. He gently put his tongue inside. I knew we would be making love tonight. He stroked my legs and continued over my entire body. He and I became one and eventually fell asleep. When I woke up in the morning, he had already had room service.

"Are you alright? No regrets from last night?"

"I thought we were one. It was beautiful. I felt like your angel."

He fed me some fruit and it was time to hit the road. We both had to work on Monday.

"We are home."

"I must have dozed off."

As usual no parking. He dropped me at the apartment and said he would call me.

*Chapter 10*

# ANTONIO ARRIVES

*I*t was about half an hour and the phone rang.
"I miss your touch already. I'd like to see you again soon. My friend Antonio is coming in from Nice, France, with his girlfriend to stay with me for a few days. I would like you to meet them." Egidio suggested.

"Let's set it up later. I need to finish some articles tonight yet, for the Times."

Tuesday night I called Laura; she was out. She called back and said,

"Peter and I were out for dinner. He isn't available much. His hours are sporadic according to how many funerals. He is nice when I can see him. It takes a special person to deal with this man's work schedule. I don't think it's me. The main question is how was your weekend at the shore?"

"Laura it was a dream. He is so attentive, complimentary, generous and gentle."

"Sounds like love to me."

"I would like to think so, but sometimes he doesn't care to talk much about his family. I know they live in Nice France and his father works for a boat company. His mother is Italian, and his father is French. That's it. I always wonder if he's hiding something."

"Call me for the next episode. I don't have your excitement."

Egidio called and said, I would like you to get together with Antonio and his girlfriend on Saturday evening at my apartment."

"Egidio, I will be able to make it Sunday, as I have some articles that have a deadline."

"Egidio said, "I will pick you up Sunday at seven. Antonio is cooking and Marjorie is assisting."

He picked me up at seven sharp, hugged and kissed me and we went. He lived in a high rise on the water. We took the elevator up to seventh floor. He opened the door and Wow!!! All contemporary, a black leather sectional, stunning large pieces of artwork on the walls in bright bold colors. Everything in order. He introduced me to Antonio and Marjorie.

"It certainly smells good."

"Antonio is a chef."

"Yes, at a small café."

"Ann don't believe him. He is the chef at one of the finest restaurants in Nice, Le Chantecler."

Antonio told we girls to go sit in the living room until the men got the dinner ready.

Antonio kidded, "Egidio can cook the pasta."

Antonio was serving Chicken Cacciatore.

The table had a white linen tablecloth, red and white striped napkins with red and white flowers in the center. I was impressed a man would have all that at hand. We ladies were seated, and the men did the presentation. Egidio poured Chianti. The conversation went into the late hours and we did drink quite a bit. Antonio suggested he and Marjorie would do the cleanup. Egidio decided to get us a cab to drop me off. We got in the back seat and kissed most of the way home. He walked me to the lobby. The cab waited for him.

Antonio and Marjorie had to leave on Tuesday, to see her aunt in New Jersey.

Egidio called on Wednesday.

"Antonio and Marjorie enjoyed our evening together and especially thought highly of my taste in a woman. I agreed. Look forward to spending more time with you next weekend. Thought we might go to the Guggenheim."

"Merci, it was a splendid evening, I agree. Gotta go and we'll talk soon."

We enjoyed the museum on the weekend.

It was a short time after I met Antonio, Egidio told me that he got a great job offer in Monaco, at Le Louis XV. He took the job and will be the chef there. This job would not be available until the current chef left in November.

*Chapter 11*

# MOM'S SURGERY

*F*riday came home from shopping and there was a message on my machine. "Call Mom."

I immediately called Mom as the message was short and to the point, I felt there was something important.

"Hi, honey, I miss you. I wanted to let you know I have going to have surgery. Don't get excited, it's a hysterectomy. I will be expected to lay low for about six weeks so if possibly you could get away, I could use some help as dad is on the road so much or he would help me. He has an important client and needs to be hands on."

"Mom now that I am no longer teaching, I am freelancing, I mainly work from home. I can bring my computer and be glad to come and be with you."

Wow change of plans for me, but being an only child, it is up to me to be there. After I hung up, I called Egidio.

"Darlin', I need to tell you; I will be away for a few weeks. My mother needs me. She is having minor surgery."

"Angel, I am sorry to hear about your mom. I will miss you to the stars, but we must be there for our parents as they were there for us. We can Facetime so I can enjoy your beautiful smile."

I flew in the day before mom's surgery. Her doctor told her it would be a routine surgery, but not to lift heavy for about six weeks. I had thought it would only be for a few weeks.

Egidio and I either talked or Facetimed every day. We missed each other seriously.

My mother and I talked about my relationship. She asked me a lot of questions. She was concerned when I said that he was vague on his parents.

"He only said that his father worked for a boat company. He seems to have some money as we go to some fancy restaurants and his apartment is furnished well. He lives in a high-rise that I am sure costs quite a bit."

"Ann be cautious. I know you like him so much. Make sure you know as much as possible about how life with him would be."

I had been with mom about three weeks and Egidio called with a quiet voice.

"Angel my love. I must leave in the morning to fly to Nice. My mother called last night, crying. She said that Papa was not well. I will miss you terribly and will be in touch. I must go to Mama. Antonio will pick me up."

# Chapter 12

# EGIDIO, PAPA NEEDS YOU

$\mathcal{A}$ntonio picked me up at the airport. He inquired, "Egidio, you have not shared with Ann that your father owns a Super Yacht company, did you?"

"No, I wanted her to like me for being me, not for my status."

"Your dad needs you, but your mother is inconsolable. I am glad you were able to get here so soon. Your mother never knew that much about the Durand Charters. She took care of the people in the office, but that's it. Sorry to say, they probably want you to take charge of the company. There are several charters going out this month. This is the season."

We arrived at my parents' home.

Mama hugged me and kissed me through tears.

"Son, I am glad you are here. I can't do this. I need to be with your Papa. I cannot take care of the business. You know all about it. I need you here. Do you want something to eat?"

Antonio and I went to the car to get my luggage.

"I see Brigette is still here. We'll talk later about that. This seems like a long-term commitment. Sounds like my life is on hold for a while. Tomorrow I'd like to come to the restaurant after you get off work and we could talk. I need to think this all through."

Antonio left and Mama and I went to Papa's room. I could see what she meant. Papa was grey in his face. He spoke.

"My son, you are here."

That was it and he fell back to sleep. Mama said he sleeps most of the time. I realized time might be short.

The next day, Mama and I talked. I went down to Durand to see what was going on at the marina. Papa hadn't been running the company for some time, but he did go in each day to see everything was running smooth.

Later for lunch, I stopped in to see Antonio at Le Chantecler. He came out of the kitchen. He was checking on the sous chef who he was training to become the chef when he left. He came to my table and said we could talk after he got off at four. We agreed he would come to Mama's house.

Antonio came over about four thirty. You would have thought we were having many guests as mama had enough food for ten. She made my favorite Lasagna, her special Italian bread and cannoli's.

After dinner, Antonio and I went down to the water and sat on the comfortable chairs each with a small glass of Amaretto.

"Antonio, I can't get a grasp on all of this. It seems I will have to stay here. You know years ago my parents wanted me to marry Camille. Her parents were French and were well healed. I tried for a short while, but I wanted an American girl who would not know my background and would love me just for being me and not for my status. I found her in Ann. I love that woman to my death. Antonio what is going to happen to me now? I can't get clarity on it."

"It will all unfold as it should. Don't walk in the fog. Just wait and it will all work out.

What's the story on Bridgette, she's been your mama's housekeeper for quite some time?"

"Oh that. One night on a summer evening, Bridgette and I were talking down at the water and my testosterone was out of control. I sat on the bench next to her, started kissing and then you know what. I wasn't that crazy about her, but the night air got to me. I never spent time with her again. I think she has always been into me that's why she agreed that night. Mama never understands why I am short with Bridgette. I want to be clear with her." Egidio lamented.

"Back to Ann. Let it decant. Don't discuss things with her until, you are sure. Does she love you?"

"I believe so, but would she move here, if that's what I need to do. You are right. I will wait to call her until tomorrow. Right now, I need some sleep."

"Call me tomorrow when you can. I didn't tell you Marjorie and I are over. She wanted me at her side every minute. I felt suffocated. We will talk about that another time. Hear from you tomorrow. Hang tight Buddy."

Egidio texted. "Ann, my love I miss you every minute. Looks like I will have to stay here for quite some time. How is your mother?"

"She is doing as she can. Operation was a success. I have been getting more assignments from the Times. They want me to go on assignment. When I return to New York, I am to go into the office for an interview for a new position. It is full time, and I would be gone from home often. I will see about it when I get back. I miss you too. Love you, bye."

*Chapter 13*

# PAPA PASSED

"How is your dad?" Ann texted Friday.

"Not well. His condition is failing. Mama really needs my support. I will call you as I can, Angel. Be well. Love you to the stars."

We talked often; I went back to New York. Mom was fine. I was busy with writing and Egidio was calling less and less.

I thought because of the distance, he might have found another interest and maybe he had had some things he wasn't willing to share with me that I needed to know.

Egidio called one day and said,

"My father passed."

He and his dad were close, he had told me; I didn't know what to say.

"Darlin', I can't imagine your sorrow. I wish I were there to hold you."

"This happened yesterday. I will call you soon. Right now, I can barely think."

I called Laura. "Egidio called. His dad passed away yesterday, and he really couldn't talk. I wonder when he is coming back. He's been distant lately, who knows maybe the love of my life is gone."

The phone rang one night, and it was Egidio.

"Angel, I need to see you so much. I will be flying in tomorrow for a week, to take care of my apartment and to hold you, if you'll see me, I know I have been less than attentive to you. I would like to explain."

Breathless I answered him. "Yes, I would enjoy seeing you."

I was a little cool wondering what he wanted to talk about.

"I would like to take you to dinner at Balthazar's and then come over to your place to talk, if you would allow me."

"Yes, that will be fine, what time will you be here?"

"Pick you up at six thirty. Bye love."

# Chapter 14

# EGIDIO'S SURPRISE

The whole conversation seemed ice cold on both sides. Wonder what the morrow will bring?

Egidio picked me up and we arrived at the quiet dinner with small talk about our families.

We both wanted to get to my house and start the real conversation. I poured a glass of wine for each of us, and he wanted us to sit on the sofa. He reached for both my hands and I felt this conversation was serious.

"Ann, my love, I need to be totally honest with you. I haven't told you, my background."

I went white. Was he a catfish or was he married or are we done?

"My parents own the Durand Super Yacht company in Nice. My grandfather had owned the company and when he passed my dad took over. I am an only child, and my mother will need me to oversee the company. It is high season soon."

I never heard of a Super Yacht but wanted to hear the rest of the story.

"I am madly in love with you and can't think of another day without you at my side. I know I have been distant lately. Trying to keep the company running is overwhelming as I had been away from home for so long. I didn't go home often while I was at Yale and then I lived in New York."

"Are you saying you are going to live in Nice permanently?"

"Yes, and I want you to come with me. This isn't the time or place for a proposal. Would you please consider it though? I know it is a huge decision. I love you so much. I didn't want to tell you about my background. I wanted to find an American girl that would love me as I am without knowing my financial status. You have loved me purely as I am, and you are all I could possibly dream of in a partner."

"It's a lot to think about, not how much I love you, but it would certainly be a total life change. I can barely speak right now."

"My love come over to me and let's hold each other for a while and be still. I adore you being in my arms.

I could not sleep at night without you by my side. The thought of losing you made me realize I better come to New York before someone else stole you. Antonio told me, "Get your ticket now. Do not wait." He could see how desolate I felt without you."

He held me and I could feel loved and cherished in every cell of my being. All my worries dissipated. Now to make some decisions.

We looked into each other's eyes and only love was between them. We loved each other to the ends of the earth.

"I am going to go now and allow you to absorb this evening."

He held me tight, we kissed, and I walked him to the door. "I love you to the moon."

He was rich and in no need of my money. What kind of home did his Mom have? If I did go, where would we live? What kind of life would we have?

And then my parents lived in Connecticut. I was their only child. I will call Mom tomorrow to run this by her. Maybe they could come visit in Nice. Would I work there? What would I do? Finally, at about three in the morning I dozed off.

Saturday morning, I called mom and told her about our talk. She was surprised Egidio was in town. I gave her the whole scoop and in her motherly way asked,

"Are you sure? Do you love him? Does he love you? If all of that is a yes, then would you enjoy France and the lifestyle it sounds like you would be living?"

"Yes, to all your queries, but I would miss seeing you and Dad."

"That is solved. We would come and visit you two. It would be nice if we could meet him. If not now, when we visit. Are you getting married?

"Mom if I decide to go, marriage is a must, maybe not this week but soon. I feel I should fly out with him when he goes, for a week or more to see if I like it and how we would be in the new setting."

"Sounds like it is reasonably decided. We love you and know we want you to be happy."

About two in the afternoon, Egidio called.

"My love, I already missed you, can we get together today and discuss more about our future, I hope together?"

"Yes darlin', I do have some more questions and love you and can't wait for you to come over. I would like it if we could order in tonight to spend all of our time together and hear what your thoughts are for our future."

"If I could fly, I'd be there in a minute, but being I have to get a cab. I'll be there in an hour, okay?"

"See you then, love you."

"That was a short hour darlin'."

"I came as soon as I could. I need you in my life every heartbeat."

We ordered Chinese and ate off each other's plates between kisses. We had a cup of Saki and opened the fortune cookies. Mine was interesting, "A Special Surprise" and his said, "Love is on the Way." It was kissing time.

"Have you thought my idea through?"

"Yes, I have. For starters, I feel I should come back with you and stay a week to see what my new life might look like. I would like to meet your mother and see what your "real" life in Nice is all about. Will I fit?"

"You definitely will fit. I am proud to introduce you to anyone. The countryside is magnificent, and I feel you would enjoy our lives there. Mama will love you and cook for you. My Italian mama loves to cook. I would love you to come with me and we can talk more about our future love life. This has all been great, but could we go lay down so I can hold you and maybe make love. I missed you so much. I need to remember how you feel."

We laid down and it was an hour later, I woke up and he was in the chair watching me sleep.

"I always love looking at you in your innocence and peace. I need to go and tomorrow I need to tell them I am not renewing my lease." I walked him to door. We hugged and kissed.

I had to call Laura. "How are you guys? Sorry I've been out of touch."

"You are not going to believe it. Lisa and Gerald got married. No big wedding. I am still going online. Peter is so unavailable with his business."

I told her my whole story.

# Chapter 15

# ANN'S TRIP TO NICE, FRANCE

"And you were the one who didn't want to go online. Maybe a catfish or wanted your money. Do you know Durand yachts rents the super yachts? They are the biggest company on the French Riviera. They rent yachts for 100-150 thousand a week." Laura said.

"I never heard of them."

"Guess you'll be one of them, Mrs. Durand."

Next day I got my ticket and surprising enough, Egidio and I got on the same flight.

Friday morning, we agreed to meet at the airport. I got to the gate and he was there.

We had a direct flight from New York to Nice. It would be about eight hours. We were not seated together. I slept most of the way, I was nervous about meeting his mom and not knowing what to expect. We got our luggage, and he had a van to pick us up. The driver was right there and said, "Mr. Durand, so good to see you."

I guess I didn't get it. He had a driver. We went through the countryside and got to what looked like an estate with a tree lined drive about a mile long. We pulled up to the circular drive and the driver let us out. The place was ornate and magnificent. Egidio ushered me to the house. Bags were still in the car. He said that Pierre would bring them into the house. An old lady came running out. Her salt and pepper hair pulled back in a bun. She had an apron on and a huge smile in her cherry pink cheeks.

"Bon Jour madam, Ann. I am so glad you could come here." She gave me a huge hug and kissed me on both cheeks. Egidio didn't have a chance to introduce me. She already seemed to know about me.

"I will make you my specialty, my Lasagna that my Egidio and his Papa always love. Come sit. I will get you a drink. You like tea?" Mama asked.

"Oh yes, my grandmother served me tea."

Egidio's Mom had rosy cheeks and a welcoming, caring smile.

After lunch Egidio asked, "Would you like to take a ride to the marina or are you exhausted from the trip?"

I was curious to see the yachts. I had no idea what I would see. We went to the marina. A huge yacht was just pulling into port. Egidio explained that two linesmen were at the dock to guide them in. When the yacht was anchored, we met the captain, and he took us on a tour. There was a huge computer room and then we saw the rest of the Yacht. I never saw that much luxury in my life. Many of the walls of the rooms were mirrored. In the halls, the walls had animal prints. Crystal chandeliers and fixtures throughout. The master bedroom had a gorgeous king bed with large windows on three sides to go to bed by starlight and wake to a sunrise. My mouth was wide open with a constant disbelief.

Egidio explained that the yachts were maintained at the Port de Saint-Tropez. To rent a yacht for a birthday party for a day would cost about $5000. He rarely took trips as he was busy with all the details. He said he did not want me to be intimidated by all this as our life would be more "normal." We would at some point go on a yacht trip as he was constantly invited. I noticed here again; everyone knew him.

I was understandably overwhelmed and out of my league. We returned to the house; I would call it a mansion. Egidio suggested I lay down and take a nap as traveling was tiring. Egidio's mom came to my room and pulled a cover over me. She had lost a daughter at birth she told me. We each had lost a daughter. Egidio went back to the dock to see how the guys had taken care of business.

When I woke, Egidio was standing over me.

"Mama thought I should bring you a cup of tea."

He kissed me on the forehead. He was curious how this revelation of his real life would affect me.

"Mama has dinner ready for us and she invited Antonio too."

She had cooked so much food. She made her special bread.

"I hope you like our food."

Mama spoke such broken English, I had to listen to every word or smile.

After dinner Mama told the three of us to go and she and Brigette would clean the kitchen. I offered and she swooshed us outside. We went down to the water and sat at the wrought iron table and chairs. Egidio had brought a bottle and some glasses, and we sipped Grand Marnier. Mama came down with a plate of macarons.

Antonio told us he met a new girl, Claire. He really likes her and hopes we will meet her.

"Come to the restaurant Saturday evening at eight as my guests. Claire will be there too. I looked to Egidio and he said,

"Of course, we'll be there."

We talked until dark and went back up to the house and Antonio drove home. Mama was already asleep, but had the bed turned back for us. We were exhausted of the beautiful day. Lights out and we made love.

The sun rose and Mama already had a plate of fruit, some baguettes and hot coffee ready.

I was only here for a week and Egidio wanted to take a drive along the water and show me around Monaco. We left after breakfast in his red Alpha Romeo convertible. He told Mama not to make dinner. We would be staying overnight at Hermitage Monte- Carlo. I am becoming spoiled. Am I going to wake up and it's all a dream? I feel like I am living the dream that my grandmother only wished she could live before she passed. Grandma, I will live it for you and me.

As we drive along the clear blue water and white sandy beaches, we barely could keep our hands off each other. Neither of us could comprehend this deep connection and heartfelt love existed. We arrived at the hotel. The interior was magnificent, European décor. Formal furniture, crystal chandeliers and oriental rugs. No surprise everyone called Egidio by name. Again, I was not entirely sure if he brought other women here in the past although I had no reason to be concerned. We went to our room to wait for our bags. Egidio threw me on the king bed and ravished me until the bellboy knocked. We decided to get ready and go sit at the beach and take a swim. We were lucky to find two lounge chairs.

"Would you like something to drink, how about a Mimosa?"

"Sounds perfect."

We lounged all afternoon and snacked. There was a beach waiter constantly passing by with different snacks, shrimp, crab on crackers and fruit.

"I think you might enjoy dinner at La Marée tonight, overlooking the bay where the yachts are docked. They have live music."

"It sounds wonderful."

"Let's take a nap before dinner. I need to hold you."

We went to the room, pulled the drapes shut and made love. We fell asleep in each other's arms.

Dinner was at nine. We both had lobster. Butter was dripping. He ordered a bottle of Sauvignon Blanc. The evening was special.

The next morning, we went down for breakfast and the ride back to Nice. Mama was there to greet us.

"Do you two want some lunch. Egidio, your Ann needs to eat more. She is so little." "Mama, girls in America want to be thin."

*Chapter 16*

# PARTY ON "THE ROSE"

We took a cheese plate and some lavender lemon drink, down to the water and sat in the shade under the huge umbrella. We recalled our day in Monaco. Neither of us cared to gamble so we missed the casinos.

Mama was in the kitchen with Brigette preparing dinner. She was preparing Carbonara.

Bridgette and Pierre always ate in the kitchen and the family always in the dining room.

Egidio had a call. Francois, an owner of one of the largest yachts was on the call.

"I am inviting you and your lady to a birthday party for my girlfriend, Tuesday on my yacht, The Rose."

Egidio answered.

"I need to talk to Ann and will let you know tomorrow."

He shared the call and I smiled. He knew I would go, but how thoughtful to ask first. I wasn't sure he would be up for socializing yet. We agreed it would be good for him to get out.

Tuesday evening, we went to the dock and had drinks and met everyone.

It was a large crowd. We boarded. The music was playing. The decorations were outstanding.

Everyone was dressed to go to a ball. Egidio knew everyone it seemed. I would have to get used to all this. It fit me well, but I would have to accept Egidio was great looking, rich and all the girls would always be after him. There was food in different areas. Each room had a theme. The food matched the theme. Seafood room was most popular. I met so many people. All of them seemed interested in who would be with Egidio. A lot of food, dancing and drinking.

We got off the yacht about two am. We got back to the house, went to our room and fell fast asleep.

Wednesday I had to pack and go back to New York.

Egidio says, "Mama doesn't want you to go. She enjoys you being here for me."

We hugged with a tear in our eyes.

"Do you have to go?" Egidio begged.

We got to the airport, kissed and hugged and agreed to talk after I got home.

It was very late Wednesday when I arrived at the apartment. Wow, a different world. Did I wake up from a dream? I loved him and how he handled himself. All that money had not gone to his head. Everyone likes him and I would have to accept that the women will be rushing to him. Good looking rich and fun. I like how he is always his own man. He cares how I feel and is always attentive to me.

Chapter 17

# ANN MAKES THE DECISION

Thursday night I had to call Laura. She is not going to believe that a lifestyle such as this, exists.

"Laura, I am back. Wow and wow. It was a fairytale lifestyle. His home is a mansion. His company is the largest yacht rental company in Nice. He is a Charter broker there. Since his father passed, he runs the company. We talked about our lives together. I want to be with him always. The only way is to live in Nice. I have been freelancing for a while. Most of my articles are online. I do need to move there."

Laura was stone quiet.

"You are sure you want to do this?"

"I have dotted all the i's and crossed all the t's and answer is yes definitely. I have already talked to my mom about this, and she said that they would come visit."

Within two weeks I was ready to go. Big decision. Mom came and we spent my last night hugging between tears. We would miss each other incessantly, but there is always Facetime and cell phones.

I caught my flight early and arrived late. The time change made it awkward, but Pierre and Egidio were at the airport. We sat in the back seat and hugged and kissed all the way home. We were like two little kids with excitement and wondering what life together for always could be like.

"I can't believe you are here. I have dreamt of you all my life and now I know who you are, Ann. You are more beautiful than in my dreams."

"You are so special. I can't believe all of this myself."

We got to the house. Egidio took me to our room. He had flowers on the nightstand. There was a little note tucked in. I opened the card. It only said, "I love you forever, Egidio."

He let me go right to sleep as the time change had me exhausted.

Morning came. Egidio was standing over our bed, smiling as always and he had a tray with a small teapot and a roll and some fruit.

It seemed he never sleeps. He is always up before me. He sat on the bed and propped the pillow behind his head and fed me the fruit sealed with a kiss.

"You are angelic when you wake up. I am so blessed that you said yes to coming here. I will take great care of you forever."

I could already smell baking downstairs.

"Is Mama already in the kitchen?"

"Yes, she and Bridgette are baking bread."

"Saturday, we are invited to go with Antonio and Claire on his sailboat. Would you like that?"

"It sounds delightful darlin'."

"Antonio is celebrating Claire's birthday. It will be fun, even more because you are with me."

We went down to greet Mama in her kitchen.

"Do you do much cooking?"

"Not too much, but I enjoy dining." Ann said.

"I will cook for you two. It is so good to have you two to enjoy my cooking."

Egidio had to check on the yachts. He said that he would be gone until midday.

"Mama and Bridgette will entertain you and take good care of you."

"Bridgette asked, "What does your family do?"

I didn't know what she meant so I answered,

"Sometimes in winter, we ski. In the summer, we go to the shore."

She looked stunned. I didn't know why she wanted to know.

"What does your father do?"

"He is an engineer."

"Oh."

Mama came into the room and offered some macarons and tea.

Egidio called. "One of the yachts has to have maintenance and it is booked for next week. I will need to be at the dock all day."

Mama suggested that Bridgette would show me the pool and the gardens. I don't know why, maybe I was nervous, but she seemed to be looking me over. I was uncomfortable. She showed me the pool and where the towels were and left me on my own. I went to the house and put my suit on and swam for almost an hour. I felt a little lost getting used to the idea, this was now my life. Egidio came back early and picked me off my feet.

"Angel, I am so sorry to have left you. I will make it up to you tonight. Let's go for a walk in the gardens. They are beautiful. I didn't realize how much I missed Nice. I hope you will like it as much as I do. I will take care to see you enjoy life with me."

"Bridgette showed me around. I felt a bit uncomfortable. She asked what my family does. I didn't know why."

"Don't pay attention to Bridgette. She lives in her own world. She can be a bit odd at times. She and

I often don't see eye to eye as long as she has been with Mama."

# Chapter 18

# CLAIRE'S BIRTHDAY PARTY

Saturday came and we had to be at the dock at four to meet with Antonio and Claire. The party started at six, but they came down to make sure the crew had everything ready. The afternoon was warm, and the breeze was gentle.

Others started to arrive, we boarded. There was plenty of seating and the drinks began to flow. I was introduced to many new people. They were all gracious. Claire got me aside and asked,

"How did you snag him?"

I froze and did not know what to say. I was aghast. A waiter passed at that moment and another girl said, "I am glad Egidio has found someone. He is such a great person. He had always been alone often. He seems happy with you."

Egidio came over and we danced until late. We arrived home about three am. We both fell asleep quickly. In the morning when I awoke, there was Egidio, a tray in hand with a pot of tea, a roll and fruit. He slid a slice of peach in my mouth.

"I love every part of you. Most of all your big brown happy eyes."

We went down and Mama and Bridgette were cooking already. Mama had come back from mass. "Tonight, I am serving you some of my special dishes. It's so nice to have you to enjoy my cooking."

Egidio held out his hand and suggested, "Come on we'll walk in the gardens."

When we turned on the path, he grabbed me and said, "Tell me last night, when I came up to you with those girls, you seemed distraught. What happened? I love you and don't want you to be uncomfortable."

Darlin', I don't know what to think, you know I love you to the ends of the earth, don't you?"

"You can't love me more than I love you. You are the world to me. Talk to me."

"Claire asked, "How did you snag him?"

"Wow. I don't know her that well, but if that's her thinking, I think Antonio should know." Egidio said.

"I don't want to start a problem. I just got here. I did not answer her. I did not know how to respond."

"Antonio, my dear friend is smart in business but never was wise in selecting his women. There was no need to respond. Come here, I want to hold you close to me. I never want you to have to deal with that again. Let me kiss you all over and know how much I love you. Let's go get some Lavender water and some cheese and fruit."

The afternoon went quickly, and it was dinner time. Mama made her version of Ravioli.

She was already becoming like a second mother. She accepted me as soon as I met her. She took Egidio aside.

"You my son love her, make an honest woman of her."

Next day, Egidio said he had to go to the dock all day. He suggested Pierre would take Mama and I to the Marc Chagall museum. He knew how much I enjoyed art. Mama said, "Ann my child, I am happy to have my girl. We only had Egidio, and I never got my girl. You are pretty for my Egidio."

"I am an only child also Mama."

While Egidio was gone, he stopped by the restaurant for lunch with Antonio. He told him what Claire had commented and when he returned, he shared with me that Antonio told him that that night a few other people made comments about Claire. They had a big fight and he told her to go figure out her life and then he would see.

Antonio said, "Marry Ann. You will never find another woman for you any better."

We were still adjusting to this new life together. He wanted to be with me and yet he had to oversee the business. I decided to make some contacts and do some freelancing. I also had started a book a while ago and started to outline it. It was a children's book on how to be an only child. I planned to have my artwork interspersed within.

The first six months was a real adjustment, I spoke extraordinarily little French. I was used to making my own bed and doing my own laundry. At this house, Bridgette did all that and Mama did all the cooking. It seems like a blessing, but it does take getting used to be taken care of completely. I told Egidio that I was feeling alone. He was gone a lot.

# Chapter 19

## COSTA RICA VACATION

"We need to take a vacation for some alone time just for us," Ann begged.

"Let's go and get married before we go. I want you forever."

We decided to go to the justice and get married. It was a nonevent because we just wanted it to be legal. We both were already madly in love.

"What do you think about this trip, A Jungle Adventure in Costa Rica?"

"That would be different, what made you think of that?"

"We need to do something we have never done and where we cannot be interrupted."

We booked the trip and in June we flew to Costa Rica. We checked in to the International Hotel and the next morning a bus picked us up and we went down to the river. We were divided into groups of six. I couldn't believe it. The boats each had a guide and we floated down the river. The water was mucky brown, and the channels were narrow. Monkeys were high in the trees and the sounds of birds was all you heard. There were many twists and turns in the river. We got off the boat at Tortuguero. We stayed a bit and then were taken down the river. We stayed at different places every night. Everything was remote. Some people lived along the way. They must go way back to town to get food by boat. Mail was delivered by boat once a week. We went to a butterfly compound all fenced in and butterflies flew on my hat and on my lips. They were all over, all colors. The main butterfly was the Blue Morpho, stunning. At another place, our boat pulled up to a Hummingbird refuge. Blue, green. Myriads of birds. Magnificent. At one stop Egidio asked me if I ever ziplined. Of course, I had not. He challenged me. We got our gear. We had to climb forty-five steps up a ladder, get hooked up and then swing over a tropical forest. He was surprised that I went. I was scared, but willing. It was great. I met his challenge.

It was a week without amenities. No cell phones, few people and just the sounds of birds and monkeys.

Time to plain enjoy nature at its purest. Only way to get around is down the river in a boat. It was an adventure.

*Chapter 20*

# Mama Passes

We arrived back to find Mama had been sick all week. We couldn't be reached in the jungle. Bridgette called in a nurse to care for her. Mama seemed to be going downhill. The doctor would come out to see her and give her some pills to make her comfortable. Mama uttered,

"Egidio my son I love you, Ann will take care of you." A few weeks later, Mama passed. Egidio went to the doctor and asked,

"How could this have happened so quick?"

"Egidio, sit down, your mother had cancer for quite some time. She did not allow me to tell you. She insisted she did not want to worry you."

I was not able to console Egidio. He sobbed and sobbed. He was thankful we got back in time to see her. We had the service just for family, we were her only family.

After that he was never the same. His sparkle was missing. We didn't make love for a couple of months. He was like a walking zombie. He was having trouble with his eyes. He had a checkup. The optometrist said his eyes were healthy, but suggested he start using eye drops each morning to keep his eyes moist.

Durand had more clients than ever, as he had improved the services and I had started redecorating the yachts inside. I started out of boredom and it was accepted so well, the company took me on payroll. I became more interested in the company and had several suggestions for Egidio.

Antonio was always there for us for anything we needed. He invited us as his guests to the restaurant. Antonio took me aside and said, "Ann, you are the best person Egidio could possibly have in his life. I hope someday to have a person such as you, for me. I am happy for my friend that you arrived in his life. I have never met a special friend as you are."

Egidio agreed to go, one of his first steps out of the house recently. Antonio was again seeing a new girl. She met us there.

"Ann and Egidio, this is Juliette."

We had an exceptional dinner. Egidio seemed to come to life.

Antonio mentioned that he and Juliette were going to Hawaii in three weeks. He begged us to go with them. I thought it would be a good idea to take Egidio's mind off his grief.

"We will have to think about it, Antonio," Ann said.

We arrived home late that night and Egidio thanked me for being kind and understanding to his feelings.

A week later Antonio called, "Egidio have you two decided to join us. Time is getting short."

*Chapter 21*

# Hawaii

"We have talked it over and Ann has convinced me I need to go."

The details were all worked out by Antonio. He was so generous. He said that we just needed to appear. We met him at the airport.

We left on a Friday morning. I sat with Juliette and Antonio said he would stay near Egidio.

Juliette was from Monaco. She said, "Antonio is the kindest man I ever met. Besides that, he is so romantic. He knows how to treat a woman."

I thought of Egidio. But I didn't care to share too much. We both dozed off most of the way.

We got off the plane and each received beautiful orchid leis. Egidio and I had lavender and white.

It seemed the trip was the exact medicine he needed. He seemed happy. He held me tight with his arm around my waist.

"You are my life saver in all of this. I can't think of anyone else I could be with at this time. You are so gentle, kind and understanding. I promise to let this week be fun for you and me. You are my life's blood right now." Egidio shared.

"You are so worth it. I will always love you. You are a part of my soul. We fell asleep. I woke up. He looked so peaceful.

"It's five. Time to wake up. We need to shower and meet them in the lobby at seven."

"Come here" as he patted the bed next to him. I need to hold you for a while."

We showered and got ready.

Dinner was romantic. We ate at the water. There were Hawaiian girl's hula dancing. The dancers were so graceful. The movements were so gentle. The night air was tranquil. It was just what we needed, some enjoyment. At the beach after dark there was a pig roast and music. There were boats out in the water with lights under the water so tourists could see the Manta Rays.

After dinner we took our shoes off and walked along the sand beach. Antonio suggested we stop for a drink at the Tiki bar. Juliette had a Mai Tai, and I had a Pina Colada inside of a pineapple with a tiny umbrella.

Next day we walked the black sand beaches. The week went fast. Time to fly back to Nice.

About a month after we returned, Egidio was still having fuzziness in his eyes. The doctor told him to keep using his eye drops and to put them in every night. He didn't need glasses.

Antonio called Egidio to ask if his eye problem was getting better and he told him Juliette and he were on different pages. She wanted to get married, and Antonio was not ready to marry so they each moved on.

I was getting to really enjoy my decision to live in Nice. I got used to this lifestyle quickly.

I called Mom to say we were back from Hawaii. She and Dad were thinking of coming to Nice soon. I would be excited to see them.

I was spending more time at the dock. I enjoyed working on the yachts. We did have people in charge of most jobs. I seemed to be changing out the interiors when needed. Some, I felt needed some updates for what clients paid to rent them.

Fall seemed to be coming too soon. Mom and Dad had set the date to come. It was only two weeks. Egidio was doing much better with his loss. He had lost both his parents within a short period of time.

Down to one week till mom and dad would come. I could barely wait.

# Chapter 22

# ANN'S FATHER AILING

om called. "Ann your father had a heart attack last night. I am nervous. The doctor said it is serious. I am scared."

"I will talk to Egidio and explain to him. I need to come home as soon as I can."

"I really do need you with me, Ann. Thanks so much."

Egidio understood after what happened to him. Pierre drove us to the airport.

Egidio texted me that the house was incredibly quiet. It was only Egidio and Bridgette. He called me every chance he had. He said, "I am lost without you. I get it, but I want to hold you. Antonio has been such a dear friend and comes over often. He just came in right now. Love you and will talk to you soon."

Antonio came in to see Egidio. "I can't believe how much you really miss Ann. I wish I could find that kind of love. I wish to have such a wonderful woman as Ann. She seems one of a kind. If ever she needs two men, I volunteer to be the second." The men laughed and talked. Antonio had an errand to run, so left shortly.

"Bridgette when you go pick up groceries, will you pick up a bottle of eye drops at the pharmacy, I'm out." Egidio asked.

Pierre drove Bridgette to the store and helped her with the groceries. They went into the pharmacy. Egidio didn't tell her which one so she asked the pharmacist which ones are best. He suggested a brand. He said, "Most brands are good as long as they have tetrahydro-zoline in, but if there are kids at home, keep it up high. If ingested, it is lethal. They picked a bottle and Pierre filled the van with gas and they went home.

"I hope these are the right eye drops." Bridgette said.

"I am sure one's as good as the other. I need some right now. My eyes are blurring."

Bridgette did all the cooking without Mama there. It was a lot for her to do the entire housekeeping. She served his coffee and roll every day, before Egidio went to the marina, Egidio told me.

I ended up being home with Mom for about two weeks. It didn't look good. Dad was not improving. One morning Mom came running into my room. "He won't wake up." We called the ambulance, but to no avail. He was gone. He had had another major heart attack.

I called Egidio and he wanted to come, but I told him it would only be Mom and I, as dad's parents were gone, and his brother Josh was out of the country. Mom's mother was gone. Mom and I would need the time to grieve. It was prime season for yacht rental also.

*Chapter 23*

# EGIDIO'S DIFFICULTIES

*E*gidio was surprised at how well Bridgette took care of his needs and how concerned she was about Ann's father and when Ann would be coming home to be with me.

After I got Mom settled, I called Egidio to tell him I was coming back to Nice. When I got back Egidio wasn't being his old self.

He started to feel nauseous occasionally and his vision continued to be blurred. He vomited one day. We thought he had the flu. He had a headache. He had shortness of breath.

We called the doctor and got an appointment the next day. The doctor checked him over and could find nothing wrong, although his blood pressure was low, and his heart rate was a little slow. He said,

"It could be a virus, as I have had a few patients recently with similar symptoms. Keep me posted if anything changes."

A couple of days went by and one day Egidio had to stay home. He slept almost all day.

The next day he was nauseous. I called the doctor and told him we needed him to come out as Egidio was too weak to get out of bed. The doctor came and checked everything and could not find much of anything. A few days later, Egidio seemed a little better. He went down to the marina for about an hour and came back. He ate lunch and then gave up his lunch. I didn't know what to do.

I called Antonio to see if he would come over. I didn't know what to do for Egidio. I needed mental support. I had to do what was needed to keep things going at the marina. He helped me with anything he could do. Moreover, Bridgette came to me and said, "It is too much for me to do everything now that Mariana has passed." I have taken another client and will be leaving next week."

*Chapter 24*

# COLETTE COMES TO LIVE

*I* called Antonio and asked him if he knew anyone or an agency I might call. He came over after work to see Egidio and he did have a name for me to interview.

"She is a young woman with experience, and I think you and she would like each other, and she does good work. Her name is Colette."

I called her the next day and told her I would be needing someone shortly. She said it was interesting that the man she housekept for, that she had been with for years passed away last month. I told her Antonio had recommended her. She told me her family and his knew each other. That made me comfortable. She said she could meet with me the next day.

She came and we instantly had rapport. She was pretty and pleasant. She did not appear to have that edge that Bridgette had.

Egidio seemed to have several bad days, and the doctor had no answers.

I asked, "Do you remember eating anything different than usual while I was gone?"

"Bridgette made a lot of the things Mama made. I don't remember anything different."

I was trying to think of anything at this point. Nothing made sense. Egidio was never sick as long as I had known him.

Moving day and Colette moved her things in. She had very pretty clothes. She needed the walk-in closet in her room. She had many hats too. As she was putting her hats on the top shelf, in the corner she found a small notebook. She came out and said, "Ma'am, I found this notebook on the top shelf. I guess the last person forgot to take it."

"You may call me Ann." I took the notebook and threw it in a drawer. It must have belonged to Bridgette, but right now I needed to attend to Egidio.

Antonio was a jewel. He came over as often as he was able to help me, whatever I needed. He helped me keep my sanity. His demeanor was always even and supportive.

The love of my life appeared to be slipping away. I thought it must be a virus and certainly soon this would all seem like a bad dream.

The next day, I went into the guest room Egidio was sleeping in lately. We thought we each would get better rest until he was feeling better, if we were in separate rooms. I shook him to wake him. He did not open his eyes. His forehead was very cool. I realized he was not breathing. I screamed and Colette came running. She said, "We need to call an ambulance now."

They came quickly and determined it appeared it was his heart. There was no pulse. They took him to the hospital although it was certain, he was gone.

Colette tells me later, I passed out. She called the doctor, and he came and gave me a sedative. Colette thought to call Antonio for help. When I came to, I was in my bed and Antonio and Colette were there.

"Where is he, where is he?" Antonio grabbed for my hand.

"Just rest Ann. Egidio is gone."

I began hysterically screaming. Antonio sat on the edge of the bed. Colette said,

"She will fall asleep shortly. The doctor has given her a sedative."

Soon Antonio and Colette went to sit in the kitchen and Ann had fallen back to sleep.

Antonio said, "We need to find Ann's mother's number and I am sure she will fly in to be with Ann.

I can't come to grips with all of this. Egidio has never been sick ever. I have known him for years. His father had a bad heart." They reached Marie and she immediately flew out.

Pierre went to the airport and picked up Mom. Mom came in the door and she said, "You do not look well, Ann. I am glad to be here for you."

"Mom, I can't imagine what happened. The doctor could find nothing. He was alright when I came to you. It is too much for both of us, with Dad passing and now this."

Ann didn't get dressed for days. She stayed in her robe and kept holding her head, saying, "no,no,no it can't have happened."

Ann did not feel an autopsy would bring Egidio back, so she opted not to have one, she figured it was his heart as his father died of his heart trouble. The death certificate said natural causes. Cremation is what Egidio had in his will, so Ann followed his wishes. The service was rather private. Ann did not want to deal with the many friends who would have come. There were so many cards, the kitchen table piled high with them. All of them saying what Egidio meant to them.

Mom stayed a week and had to go back to take care of her house. She was in the process of selling it. I was still on medication to keep me going.

Antonio was a very special friend. He came mostly on the weekends as he lived in Monaco now near his job. He helped me with all the paperwork that needed to be changed over. When Egidio's Mom passed, we had to change the company papers all over to Egidio. Egidio had a new will made to leave everything to me if he passed before me. Never did we think much about it. We were both young, at least to die.

Colette was a god sent. She waited on me hand and foot and listened to my every word. She was such a comfort.

Antonio came over one weekend, and he needed a pen to write some directions for me to contact different people to assist me. I opened the drawer and he asked,

"What's that notebook?"

"Oh, that's a notebook Bridgette left on a shelf in her room. I'll have to send it to her."

"Did you ever look what's in it?"

"Not really."

Antonio out of curiosity turned a few pages. He didn't want me to see it and laid it down.

Now I was curious. He seemed to abruptly put it down. I picked it up and read a few lines, I couldn't believe it. "She loved him and hated me for taking Egidio from her. She believed he belonged to her. I can't read any more. This scares me."

"You don't think she would do anything, do you?"

"No, I always felt she didn't care for me, but nothing more."

The next week Antonio offered to take me to where Bridgette lived to deliver the notebook.

We dropped over. Bridgette came to the door. She seemed to be home alone. I had the notebook in my hand. She went white and her face was blank.

"You didn't read my private stuff, did you?"

"Bridgette, yes we did."

Antonio and I stared as she started to react.

"It was all your fault, Ann. Until you came along, I still thought there was a chance. I loved him first. He was mine."

"Bridgette, you had no right to take the love of my life. Did you harm him?"

She looked at the floor saying nothing.

Antonio immediately insisted, "We need to call the authorities."

Bridgette sat on a chair at the table and got hysterical. She cupped her hands over her eyes and put her head on the table. "I loved him, I loved him and then you came along. It's not fair. He belonged to me."

Antonio had called and the police came right away. Antonio had given them some background on our story. They sat her down and tried to talk to her, but she stayed hysterical. They took her by the hand and led her out. They said that they would be in touch after they spoke with her.

Ann was beside herself. She couldn't believe there might be foul play. She never got along that well with Bridgette, but what could have happened.

Antonio came back to the house with me. I was totally a mess by now. He asked me if I wanted to talk or go lie down. I said that I wouldn't be able to rest.

"You know when I think about it, when I left to go to Mom's, Egidio was fine, just fuzzy eyes. He had eye drops for that. It's when I came back, he started to be sick."

"Did he have anything out of the ordinary to tell you like what he ate or drank that was unusual?"

"I asked him all that and he said, "No."

The next day, the police department officer called and asked me to come in and if Antonio would be available also, he should come. They wanted as much information as possible. Bridgette was being held because from how she was acting, they thought to place her on suicide watch.

She had kept telling them, "I had to do it." She would never say what or how.

Antonio was able to come with me. I told them the story as I knew it. I never thought Egidio's death was anything other than natural.

The officers had a psychologist working with Bridgette. She did not make a lot of sense. Her stories changed moment to moment. They told me they would get back to me as soon as they had talked more with Bridgette.

About a week later, the officer called me into his office. He asked me if Egidio has been taking any medication. I told him no, the very only thing he had since I met him was recently. He had problems with his eyes and had taken eye drops. The death certificate stated natural causes. Does anyone else live in your home?

"No family members. I do have a driver Pierre and a housekeeper Colette. Colette came recently, but Pierre has always been there as long as I have." Ann answered.

"We will need to speak with Pierre, only to cover all bases. He may have some new information."

"Okay, but I don't think he will know anything. He is an incredibly private man. He is a fine worker. He keeps to himself and never says much."

Pierre was able to go to the authorities and talk with them. The only thing he knew was picking up the eye drops for Egidio and the pharmacist not helping them pick out a definite brand, but said, "Don't let little kids get it. If they ingest it, it could be lethal."

Antonio after hearing about the eye drops, looked into articles about eye drops and discovered if ingested a person could die.

"Ann, I looked up eye drops, and they can be killers if you take them internally."

"That would make sense due to the timing because when I left to go to Mom, Egidio was healthy. It makes me sick to think about, but nothing will bring my Egidio back."

After a series of interviews, the authorities and the psychologist determined that Bridgette needed to go to a mental facility. They said without evidence or proof there would be no case, but Bridgette has severe mental issues and needed serious counseling. She never said anything other than, "I needed to do it." Never did she explain how or why or what she did.

I was too exhausted from the whole thing and nothing would bring Egidio back. I had to go on never knowing what might have happened. I decided to bury myself in my work to carry on.

## Chapter 25

# ANTONIO RETURNS

*A*ntonio nor I needed money. I needed to work to keep me going. I learned to enjoy the yacht company so much that I wanted to keep it going.

I called Antonio on Friday and invited him to dinner. Colette would be making Cordon Bleu. I already knew I had ulterior motives. He agreed to come.

Colette was such a delight, I wished Egidio could have got to know her better. After dinner, Colette left us to talk.

"Would you like some Grand Marnier?"

"That would be great."

"I do need to admit, I had a reason to invite you tonight. I feel like I want to keep the company. I have learned a lot and enjoy working. I'd like you to give it some thought. Egidio has told me how you were such an asset to him at the dock. I would like you to be the chief operating person. I know you have your sailboat and know a lot about the yachts. No need to answer me now as I know it's a lot being you have a fulltime job."

"Ann, what you don't know is that I am planning to come back from Monaco. I love Nice and want to live here. It's not as farfetched as you think. I have always loved being able to see you as much as possible. I love the water and the yachts.

Would you like to come to Monaco next weekend? I would get a room for you. You would be my guest at the restaurant. I realize we are just friends, but I would enjoy your company and I feel you really need a weekend away from your sorrows."

"Yes, I would enjoy that. Maybe by then, you will have thought about my proposition."

I was looking forward to the coming weekend. The Louis XV restaurant was well known by our friends. The hotel was fabulous. My heart was beating. I had thought for quite some time about getting away for a while. I even was deciding what clothes to pack. It wasn't a romantic relationship, but I did love Antonio for all he was to Egidio and now what he means to me to be there for me in my darkest hours.

I decided to take the train to Monaco. I took a cab from the station. He told me to call him when I arrived.

Antonio met me in the lobby. The concierge was instructed that I was his guest and to take care of my needs. He said he would be off work at four and call my room.

I went down early to look around. There were gold ornate gilded walls, chandeliers dripping with crystals. Marble busts throughout, oil murals and tall windows draped by ivory valances that were breathtaking.

We met at seven. Everyone knew Antonio as everyone had known Egidio. We were seated at the Chef's table.

Antonio admiringly glanced. I had a red, short spaghetti strap dress and red strappy shoes.

Dinner was beautiful. I say beautiful because the presentations were superb.

After dinner, Antonio suggested we walk through the gardens. There were paths with low lighting.

We talked about how we appreciated each other.

"Let us go and have an after-dinner drink. There is a table here in the garden, the waiter will come to us."

The moon was full this night. Antonio ordered two glasses of Cointreau.

We raised our glasses to peaceful times ahead.

"I know I need to answer your question, but later not to waste the ambiance. Ann, I need to share with you that I love you as well as Egidio loved you. He shared all your attributes and as I got to be around you, I saw for myself how beautiful a soul you are. I am trying not to be inappropriate, but these are my feelings."

"I thought it was only me, but my feelings have been similar. You have always been a great friend to Egidio, and he shared with me, your huge heart, your beautiful soul and since he is gone, I have experienced you for myself."

"Oh, maybe we should walk down to the water. This conversation is intense."

We walked awhile and decided to go to the lounge.

Antonio suggested we have a glass of wine before we said good night.

"Now to my question, what is your decision?"

"I have seriously thought of it and I believe we will make a good team, so the answer is YES."

I got off my seat and grabbed him and kissed him.

"I apologize, I got so excited that you would come."

"No need to apologize. Would you like to try that again?"

Antonio walked me to my room. We hugged and he left.

Next day, I caught the train back to Nice.

Antonio texted. "I had a wonderful time spending it with you. I hope you had a relaxing evening too. Is there the possibility we could do that again?"

Antonio, I would like you to come to Nice next weekend if you are available to look over the business. You could stay in one of the guest rooms, rather than driving back. I will make plans for us to dine on Saturday evening. Let me know if that works for you."

Antonio responded rather quickly and agreed to come.

Saturday morning Antonio arrived. Pierre met him and carried in his bag and parked his car. I looked out the windows and saw a gorgeous red car. I took Pierre aside and asked," Pierre what is that?"

Pierre said," It is a Bugatti Chiron."

Not that I knew what that meant.

Antonio was looking around outdoors. "The gardens are magnificent."

"Pierre oversees them."

Antonio came in. We hugged and he said that traffic was horrific today.

Saturday when he arrived, we went down to the dock and I explained the company details.

# Chapter 26

## ANTONIO OVERSEES DURAND

*A*ntonio hesitantly said, "I always knew Egidio was always thinking of the crew and the guests. I told him often, he needed to get someone in charge of the numbers. I have agreed to live in Nice and be part of this company. However, I know you love him, but you need to address the numbers. Ann, you have the best yachts with guests with the most money. You need to charge appropriately. I know I sound harsh, but I now am speaking business. You know I love you, that's why I need to speak clearly."

"Antonio, you are only saying what I already knew. Egidio had such a big heart. That is why everyone that knew him loved him, including me. That is a determent to all business. We will make a great team because we are on the same page."

"Ann let's give it a rest and I will take you to lunch. La Tartane has great food."

"I agree, I think we agree with the business. Thank you so much for your honesty and for helping me out."

After lunch, we relaxed at my place down near the water and gardens. The fountain was a pleasant relaxing sound in the background. Pierre had done a lot of the landscape design.

It was exquisite. We sat at the gazebo. Colette brought us some Citron Presse. I call it Lavender Lemonade.

That evening I had made reservations at La Cucina. Pierre dropped us off and would come back later.

Antonio ordered a bottle of Pinot Noir. I enjoyed Duck ala Orange and Antonio had Glazed Salmon. The evening was romantic in its own way. He treated me well, was such a gentleman and I was beginning to feel the scent of love.

Pierre arrived and we went to my home.

"Let's sit outdoors. It is a lovely evening to inhale the scents of the gardens," Antonio suggested.

"Would you like some Baileys?

"Yes, that would be special with you."

We talked about Egidio. "It feels as though you and he are brothers from different mothers. I feel so close to you. You have been supportive of me as long as I have known you."

"I feel the same about you."

"It is getting late; I will show you to your room."

Colette had already gone to her room.

As I stood at the door of Antonio's room. He grabbed me and kissed me. I did not back away, and it became a long kiss.

"I apologize. I already am in love with you. I apologize only because I didn't ask."

"I didn't back away, did I? Sleep well."

Colette had the breakfast table set and coffee brewing.

"Colette you are such a pleasant edition to my home. I would be lost without you here.

Antonio came out to the kitchen. "I smell coffee."

For a minute I felt like he already lived here, and we were together. I shook it off. Where did that come from?

Antonio and I spent the day at the marina and talked about the changes we agreed on.

Antonio suggested he would cook for Colette and me this evening. He created a dish which we enjoyed.

Colette suggested we go outdoors, and she would finish in the kitchen.

We talked for hours and then it was late so we agreed that Antonio would stay over and drive home on Monday. We each wanted to spend more time.

I walked Antonio to his room.

"Would you like to come lay down for a while?

I followed him. We laid down, held each other and fell asleep.